The Matzah That Papa Brought Home

by **FRAN MANUSHKIN**

Illustrated by **NED BITTINGER**

SCHOLASTIC INC.

New York · Toronto · London · Auckland · Sydney

Special
thanks to
Rabbi Melinda Panken
for fact-checking the manuscript.

ISBN 0-590-82903-3

Text copyright © 1995 by Fran Manushkin.
Illustrations copyright © 1995 by Ned Bittinger.
All rights reserved. Published by Scholastic Inc.

12 11 10 9 8 7 6 5 4 3 2 1   3   6 7 8 9/9 0 1/0

Printed in the U.S.A.   14

Designed by Marijka Kostiw

Ned Bittinger's artwork
was rendered in oil paint
on linen.

THIS IS THE MATZAH that Papa brought home.

THIS IS THE FEAST that Mama made
with the matzah that Papa brought home.

THIS IS THE PASSOVER SEDER we shared
to eat the feast that Mama made
with the matzah that Papa brought home.

THIS IS ME standing tall and proud
to ask the Four Questions nice and loud
during the Passover Seder we shared
to eat the feast that Mama made
with the matzah that Papa brought home.

THESE ARE THE PLAGUES that we counted — all ten —
by dipping our pinkies again and again
after I stood up tall and proud
and asked the Four Questions nice and loud
during the Passover Seder we shared
to eat the feast that Mama made
with the matzah that Papa brought home.

THIS IS "DAYENU," a very long song
that we sang with our stomachs growling along
after we counted the plagues — all ten —
by dipping our pinkies again and again
after I stood up tall and proud
and asked the Four Questions nice and loud
during the Passover Seder we shared
to eat the feast that Mama made
with the matzah that Papa brought home.

THESE ARE THE BITTER HERBS that we dipped
after *"Dayenu,"* a very long song
that we sang with our stomachs growling along
after we counted the plagues — all ten —
by dipping our pinkies again and again
after I stood up tall and proud
and asked the Four Questions nice and loud
during the Passover Seder we shared
to eat the feast that Mama made
with the matzah that Papa brought home.

THIS IS THE MATZAH BALL SOUP that we sipped
after the bitter herbs that we dipped
after *"Dayenu,"* a very long song
that we sang with our stomachs growling along
after we counted the plagues — all ten —
by dipping our pinkies again and again

after I stood up tall and proud
and asked the Four Questions nice and loud
during the Passover Seder we shared
to eat the feast that Mama made
with the matzah that Papa brought home.

THIS IS THE AFIKOMAN I found
by searching the house and running around,
after the matzah ball soup that we sipped
after the bitter herbs that we dipped
after *"Dayenu,"* a very long song
that we sang with our stomachs growling along
after we counted the plagues — all ten —
by dipping our pinkies again and again
after I stood up tall and proud
and asked the Four Questions nice and loud
during the Passover Seder we shared
to eat the feast that Mama made
with the matzah that Papa brought home.

THIS IS THE DOOR we opened wide
inviting Elijah to step inside
after the *afikoman* was found
by searching the house and running around,
after the matzah ball soup that we sipped
after the bitter herbs that we dipped
after *"Dayenu,"* a very long song
that we sang with our stomachs growling along
after we counted the plagues — all ten —
by dipping our pinkies again and again
after I stood up tall and proud
and asked the Four Questions nice and loud
during the Passover Seder we shared
to eat the feast that Mama made
with the matzah that Papa brought home.

Finally, "NEXT YEAR IN JERUSALEM!" WE SAID,
then everyone hugged, and went to bed,
after the door was opened wide
inviting Elijah to step inside
after the *afikoman* was found
by searching the house and running around,
after the matzah ball soup that we sipped
after the bitter herbs that we dipped
after *"Dayenu,"* a very long song
that we sang with our stomachs growling along
after we counted the plagues — all ten —
by dipping our pinkies again and again
after I stood up tall and proud
and asked the Four Questions nice and loud
during the Passover Seder we shared
to eat the feast that Mama made
with the matzah that Papa brought home.

Now the Passover moon shines its beams,
bringing the children of Israel sweet dreams . . .
and we will remember the stories and matzahs
our mamas and papas brought home.

The Story of Passover

T HOUSANDS OF YEARS AGO IN EGYPT, a cruel pharaoh enslaved the Jewish people. When Moses, the leader of the Jews, went to Pharaoh and asked him to "Let my people go," Pharaoh refused.

But the Jewish people did not give up! And through their faith in God, after years of slavery, Moses led them out of Egypt to freedom. The story of this miraculous exodus is told every spring during the holiday of Passover.

Passover lasts for eight nights and seven days. On the first and second nights, families and friends gather together at dinners, called "Seders." Reading from a book called a *"Haggadah"* (which means the "telling"), they reenact the ancient drama. This is done by asking and answering questions, singing and praying, and tasting special foods and wine.

These rituals and foods help all the people at the Seder feel as if the exodus were happening to them, as if they, too, were freed from slavery in Egypt. Indeed, all the people at the Seder know that they are free people today because of their ancestors' courage so long ago.

Here are some of the foods and rituals of the Seder:

Matzah: This is the "bread of affliction" — unleavened bread. After Pharaoh finally agreed to let the Jewish people go, he insisted that they leave that very night! Because the Jews departed so quickly, there was no time to add yeast to their bread and wait for it to rise. So the bread they took out of Egypt was flat and unleavened. That is why, during the Passover holiday, only unleavened bread is eaten. Dumplings are made out of matzah, and these are called "matzah balls."

Green Vegetable: This green is a reminder of spring, the Passover season. It is dipped in salt water to symbolize the salty tears of the Jewish slaves. In most cases, people choose parsley as the green vegetable.

Roasted Egg: The egg is a symbol of the animal sacrifice that was brought to the Temple for each festival. The egg is also a symbol of life, and it is eaten to symbolize the Jewish people coming to life as a nation.

Shank Bone: This is a reminder of the lambs that the ancient Jews used to offer as a sacrifice to God every spring.

The Four Questions: These are asked by the youngest child at the Seder, first in Hebrew and then in English. They are:

1. Why is this night different from all other nights? On all other nights, we eat leavened or unleavened bread. Why, on this night, do we eat only matzah, which is unleavened?

2. On all other nights we eat various vegetables. Why, on this night, must we eat bitter herbs?

3. On all other nights we need not dip our herbs. Why, on this night, do we dip twice? (We dip the green vegetable in salt water and the bitter herbs in *haroset.*)

4. On all other nights we eat sitting up. Why, on this night, do we recline at the table?

(You will find the answers to the first three questions by reading the descriptions under *Matzah, Bitter Herbs, Green Vegetable,* and *Haroset.* The answer to the fourth question is that, since the Jewish people are no longer slaves, they may recline at dinner — just as royalty used to do!)

Wine: Jewish holidays always begin by reciting a blessing and drinking a cup of wine. On Passover we drink four cups of wine to symbolize the four divine promises that are found in the Book of Exodus. These promises are: "I will bring you out. I will deliver you. I will redeem you. I will take you to me."

The Ten Plagues: When Pharaoh refused to free the Jews, God commanded Moses to tell Pharaoh that if he did not release them, God would send down a terrible plague. But Pharaoh refused, and God turned the rivers to blood. When Pharaoh saw this, he promised to free the Jews, but then he went back on his word. So God sent a plague of frogs. Again Pharaoh promised to free the Jews and then went back on his word. Each time Pharaoh broke his promise, a new plague would descend on him and his people. Today, as the name of each plague is read during the Seder, everybody dips a finger into a wineglass and removes a drop of wine. We do this to diminish the pleasure of the drink, for how can anyone be happy when some of God's children suffered so terribly?

The first nine plagues were: blood, frogs, lice, wild beasts, pestilence, boils, hail, locusts, and darkness. The tenth and last plague was the worst: the death of all the firstborn sons of the Egyptians. The homes of Jewish families were "passed over," sparing them. This is the origin of the name "Passover."

Pharaoh finally told the Jews that they could go. But again he changed his mind and sent his great army after them. When the Jews reached the Red Sea, God created a miracle: The sea divided, and the escaping Jews walked on dry land, between two walls of water. When the Egyptian army pursued them, the walls of water rushed together again, and the army perished.

"Dayenu": This is a song with fourteen choruses, expressing gratitude for fourteen of God's gifts. (The word *"dayenu"* means "it would have been enough.") This song says that if God had done just one of these things it would have been enough, but God kept on doing more and more!

Bitter Herbs: Usually this is horseradish. Its bitter taste is a reminder of the bitterness of slavery.

Haroset: This is a mixture of apples, nuts, wine, and spices. It symbolizes the mortar the Jewish slaves used to make the bricks for Pharaoh's pyramids and cities.

Afikoman: This is a piece of matzah that is hidden at the start of the Seder. Near the end of the Seder, all the children search for the *afikoman*, and whoever finds it receives a prize.

Cup of Elijah: At the end of the Seder a door is opened, in the hope that Elijah, a great prophet, will come and drink the wine that has been poured into a cup for him. When Elijah comes, there will be peace among all peoples on earth. Children check the cup carefully to see if any of the wine has been drunk.

Finally, everyone says, "NEXT YEAR IN JERUSALEM!" These words had special meaning when the Jewish people were scattered all over the world and could not return to Israel. Today, those who are celebrating Passover in the state of Israel say, "NEXT YEAR IN A JERUSALEM REBUILT!"

After the Seder, when the children go to sleep, they know they will have more days of the Passover holiday to look forward to — and they will always remember the story of Passover.